SAURUS STREET

A Plesiosaur Broke My Bathtub

SAURUS STREET

A Plesiosaur Broke My Bathtub

Nick Falk and Tony Flowers

RANDOM HOUSE AUSTRALIA

To Geoff, for his patient proofing, and to Mum and
Dad, for their endless encouragement — Nick Falk

For Nelly, my much loved and much missed
grandmother — Tony Flowers

A Random House book
Published by Random House Australia Pty Ltd
Level 3, 100 Pacific Highway, North Sydney NSW 2060
www.randomhouse.com.au

First published by Random House Australia in 2013

Addresses for companies within the Random House Group can be found at
www.randomhouse.com.au/offices

National Library of Australia
Cataloguing-in-Publication Entry

Author: Falk, Nicholas
Title: A plesiosaur broke my bathtub / Nick Falk; Tony Flowers, Illustrator
ISBN: 978 0 85798 182 0 (pbk)
Series: Falk, Nicholas. Saurus street; 5
Target Audience: For primary school age
Subjects: Plesiosaurs – Juvenile fiction
Other Authors/Contributors: Flowers, Tony
Dewey Number: A823.4

Cover and internal illustrations by Tony Flowers
Internal design and typesetting by Anna Warren, Warren Ventures
Printed in Australia by Griffin Press, an accredited ISO AS/NZS 14001:2004 Environmental
Management System printer

Random House Australia uses papers that are natural, renewable and recyclable products and made
from wood grown in sustainable forests. The logging and manufacturing processes are expected to
conform to the environmental regulations of the country of origin.

CHAPTER ONE
The Witching Hour

There are three reasons I'm scared of Granny and Grandad's outdoor loo.

1. The door might close and leave me locked inside forever.
2. Every creepy-crawly in the whole wide world lives in there.
3. (and the big reason) The toilet has no bottom.

It's not like a normal toilet, with water and a U-tube. Granny and Grandad's toilet is just a hole over a big black pit. Anything could be hiding down there. Like a witch or a werewolf. Or a hideous green water monster with **gigantic** teeth.

I don't consider myself a scaredy-cat. I'm nine years old and I wear size 7 shoes. And that's big

for my age. But only a fool wouldn't be scared of that toilet.

I tiptoe slowly down the garden path. I always go slowly just in case the witches and werewolves have forgotten to hide. That way I might see them and have time to run away. But there's nothing to see. Just a creepy cabin hidden in the trees.

Granny and Grandad live in the oldest house on Saurus Street. It's ancient. Even older than they are. It's so old it doesn't even have **electricity**. If you want light, you have to use a candle or a torch. And there's no indoor loo.

Grandad says they'd have to dig up the floor and put in pipes to make

an indoor loo. He says that would cost a 'pretty penny'. And Grandad doesn't have a pretty penny. So the only loo they have is the one in the garden.

I only stay with Granny and Grandad one weekend a month. I love it.

But I'm terrified of that toilet.

During the day I don't mind it. It's quite *fun*. You can hide in there and

pretend you're in
an alien spaceship
flying to Mars.
But at night it

SCARES
the pants off
me. And my
bladder always wakes me up at midnight,
needing to go. Midnight – **the witching hour**. My bladder
must hate me.

I reach the toilet door. It's rattling
on its chain, almost like it's alive. I take
a deep breath, and pull it open.

But there's nothing there.

Just a seat, a black pit and five
million mosquitoes. Granny and
Grandad's house is built on top of a

stinky smelly swamp. It's about the worst place anyone could live on Saurus Street. But mosquitoes love it. They think it's paradise.

I step into the toilet. Immediately the door bangs shut. Just the wind, that's all. No need to *panic*. I take another deep breath, count to five and

pull down my pyjama pants. It's going to be okay. In two minutes I'll be back in bed. There's nothing in here, nothing to be scared of . . .

SPLASH!

Something moved. Deep down in that dark black pit.

I freeze, every hair on my body standing on end.

SSSSS.

I can hear something *slithering* around down there, rising up towards me.

I close my eyes and take a breath. It's okay. There's nothing there. It's just my imagination. I've got a very powerful imagination. So powerful it sometimes makes me hear things that aren't real.

I start feeling calmer. This will all be over soon. And tomorrow morning it'll be Saturday. Weekend! And weekends are brilliant –

tOOOOMAAAAAs

There's a voice. Coming from the toilet. Saying my name.

tOOOOMAAAAas

I can't believe it. There really is a monster down there. And it knows I'm here. It's coming up to eat me!

I scramble backwards, heart beating like a drum. I need to get out of here. Fast.

I push against the door. *But it's stuck! It won't budge!*

This really is the end!

toooOOOOMAAAAs

I think about screaming, but I can't remember how. I can see a shape,

rising out of the darkness. It's some sort of head . . .

IT'S THE HIDEOUS GREENWATER BEAST FROM MY NIGHT-MARES. MY IMAGINATION HAS MADE IT COME TRUE!

I turn around and boot the door as hard as I can. It opens. I look behind me.

The head is almost above the toilet seat. I don't stop for my pyjama pants. I just run and run and run. Down the garden path, through the back door, up to bed and straight under the covers.

That does it. I'm never going to the toilet again.

CHAPTER TWO
Something Alive Down There . . .

Grandad's sitting at the breakfast table reading a letter.

'Blasted Parsnips,' he growls.

'Ooh parsnips, I do enjoy parsnips,' croons Granny, as she spreads mustard on her toast. She's a bit **odd**, my gran.

'Not parsnips, *Parsnips*,' snaps

Grandad, slamming the letter onto the table. 'Those blasted Parsnips are threatening to have our house knocked down!'

Reverend Parsnip and his wife, Priscilla, come from the posh end of Saurus Street. The end that's not in the middle of a **swamp**. They want to build a big shiny fishing lodge near Lake Saurus for rich tourists. And Grandad's house is right where they want to build it.

'It's disgraceful,' barks Grandad, 'they've got no right to threaten me. I fought in two world wars!'

Grandad used to be a soldier. He's got loads of medals, and that means he was **very brave**. I'm proud of my grandad.

'Would you like some toast, sweetie?' chirps Gran, passing me the mustard.

'No thanks, Gran,' I say.

'Maybe some bacon and eggs then?' she says. Gran gets up and wanders over to the stove.

You have to be careful with Granny's cooking. It can be a bit

EXPLOSIVE.

Last month she gave me fish fingers with hot chilli sauce (she thought it was tomato sauce). It almost blew my head off.

Grandad snatches his spoon and starts **slurping** up his cereal. Coco Pops with hot coffee. Granny almost got it right. He's still muttering to himself about Parsnips. Now's my chance.

'Er . . . Grandad,' I say, 'could I ask you something?'

Grandad doesn't reply. He's a bit hard of hearing. Especially when he's **angry**.

'Grandad,' I say a bit louder, 'I want to ask something.'

'You've been asked to sing?' barks Grandad, spraying Coco Pops across the table. 'Who by?'

'Not sing,' I say. 'Some*thing*. I want to ask some*thing*!'

'You've lost a ring?' he asks. 'Where?'

'The toilet,' I say. 'I think there's something down there.'

'In the toilet? You dropped the ring down there?' Grandad shakes his head. 'Well, that's the end of it, I'm afraid. Deep as a well, that toilet. You'll never

find it in there.' He goes back to his cereal.

I take a deep breath and speak as **clearly** as I can. 'I THINK . . . THERE'S SOMETHING ALIVE . . . IN THE TOILET.'

Suddenly Grandad smiles. 'Ah!' he says. 'Something alive! In the toilet! Why didn't you say so in the first place?' He starts pouring yoghurt into his coffee cup. 'It's probably some kind of **animal**,' he adds.

'That toilet's built over an old sinkhole. It's been there for a hundred and fifty years. Who knows how deep it is? There could be anything down there.' He gives me a grin. 'Don't sit down for too long, that's my advice. Just in case

it **POPS** up to say hello.'

CHAPTER THREE
Into the Darkness

I open my eyes and look at the clock.

Midnight.

The witching hour.

It's time to go.

I take a deep breath and get out of bed. I'm scared, but I'm also prepared. I've spent the whole day getting ready.

I open my bag and check that

everything I need is still inside. Great big torch, night goggles and a whistle in case things get nasty.

If there's a monster in the toilet, I'm ready for it. The light in my torch is extra bright, and  the night goggles have got new batteries in. I'll be able to see the monster as soon as it jumps out and tries to eat me.

And what's more, I've got a brand-new camera. I'm going to get  photographic evidence that it's real. And then I'll be in the newspaper. 'World's Greatest Monster Catcher.' That's what

they'll call me. I'll be **famous**.

Of course, what I'm really hoping for is a dinosaur. I love dinosaurs. I think they're brilliant. I've loved them since I was tiny. And I'm VERY ANNOYED

that a **giant** meteor wiped them out 65 million years ago. What did it have to go and do that for?

Of course, if there is a dinosaur in the toilet, it won't be an actual dinosaur. It will be a plesiosaur. Plesiosaurs lived at the same time as dinosaurs, but they had fins instead of legs, and they

lived in water. They were awesome. Unfortunately, plesiosaurs were wiped out too. Stupid meteor.

But the monster in the toilet isn't a plesiosaur. I know that. Because not only do plesiosaurs no longer exist, it seems that this monster knows my name. Did I make it appear with my **imagination**? The only water monster in my imagination is the huge green one with gigantic teeth I have nightmares about. So I'm guessing that's what's living in the toilet.

I tiptoe downstairs and open the back door. First of all I check for witches. Those are the other things that lurk in

my imagination. And my imagination is clearly pretty **powerful** at the moment.

I turn on the torch and shine it around the garden. Nope. No witches. Good. One imaginary monster is quite enough to deal with, thank you very much.

I start **creeping** towards the toilet. I wonder if the monster's already waiting for me? I've been thinking about it all evening, so it must know I'm coming. I wonder if it's brought any friends along? I hope not.

I put my hand on the toilet door. I take a deep breath.

One, two, three, GO!

I push it open quickly. Nothing.

The monster's not here yet. Maybe it got delayed?

I tiptoe *slowly* towards the toilet. I lean over it very carefully and shine the torch down the hole.

All I can see is blackness. This toilet must go all the way to the earth's core. Maybe there's lava down there? Maybe

one day it'll **ERUPT** and Saurus Street will turn into a gigantic volcano? That really would be cool.

I take off my bag and reach for my camera. I need to move quietly so I can hear the monster as soon as it comes. I don't want to be taken by surprise.

Suddenly I hear a noise behind me. I spin around.

There's a crooked black figure standing in the doorway, silhouetted by the moon. It looks like an old woman wearing a long pointy hat and a cloak.

'Who's there?' it croaks.

I can't believe it.

MY IMAGINATION HAS MADE A WITCH!

The witch reaches out towards me. She's going to take me to her cave! She'll cook me in her cauldron and eat me!

'Noooo,' I gurgle.

I stumble away from her and the back of my knee knocks into the toilet. I lose my balance and start falling sqɿɐʍʞɔɐd, my arms spiralling in the air.

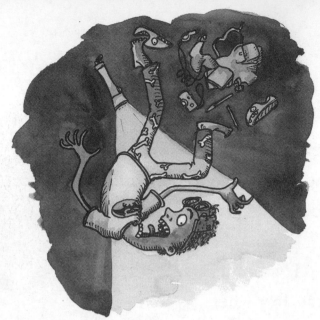

The witch steps closer. 'Thomas,' she says, 'is that you?' The moonlight hits her face.

It's not a witch. It's just Granny, wearing her nightgown and long pointy night cap.

But it's too late to stop myself. I topple over, right through the hole and tumble down into the murky darkness below.

CHAPTER FOUR
Hooked!

I seem to fall forever. This must be the deepest toilet in the world. And just when I'm certain I really have reached the earth's core . . . **SPLASH!** I plunge into icy cold water.

Thank goodness it wasn't lava.

It's pitch black. I can't see a thing. I can't even see my hand in front of my face. And the water is so deep I can't touch the bottom.

'Gran!' I shout. 'Granny!'

But there's no answer. Granny's gone. No-one can hear me. I'm stuck, trapped down here with the water beast. I'm hoping it's a herbivore and only eats plants.

I swim over until I can feel the walls. Maybe I can climb up? But they're smooth and **STICKY** with mud. At least I hope it's mud. This is a toilet after all. Yuck.

I try climbing but I can't. And the opening's too far anyway.

I look around me. My eyes are starting to adjust to the darkness. On three sides of me are walls, and on the other side is an underwater tunnel. There's a faint light coming from the end of it.

The tunnel's my only chance. I'm going to have to swim through it. Luckily I'm a good swimmer. I came second in the Year 4 backstroke race this year. And I only lost because Sally Simpson cheated. (She wore invisible fins.)

I take a deep breath and dive under the water. It's so cold it feels like I'm swimming through ice. I push as hard as I can with my arms and legs, and slowly I swim closer to the light. It feels like my lungs are about to **burst**,

but I think I'm going to make it.

Suddenly I look up and realise I'm not in the tunnel anymore. I can see the moon shining through the water high above me. I've swum out into Saurus Lake. I'm alive!

I kick upwards, swimming for the surface. My lungs are desperate for air, and I'm almost there when . . . TUG.

Something's pulling on my pyjamas. Panic floods through me. I try to pull away, but the hold's **too strong**.

The sea monster's got me. Just like in my nightmares. My final moments have come.

I struggle and **squirm**, but the monster won't let go. It drags me kicking and screaming through the water. I close my eyes, waiting for teeth to sink into my flesh.

SPLOSH!

The monster pulls me right out of the lake. And leaves me there, **dangling** and dripping in the cold night air.

'You're not a squid,' says the monster.

I turn my head. There's a little rowing boat beside me. And inside the boat is a girl with bright red hair. She's holding a fishing rod in her hands, and she's looking at the thing she's just hooked on the end of her line.

And that thing is me.

CHAPTER FIVE
The Loch Saurus Monster

I sit there **shivering** in the boat. The girl ignores me as she busily sticks a worm on her fishing line.

'What are you doing out here?' I say. It's the middle of the night. And she only looks about one or two years older than me.

'Shhh,' whispers the girl. 'You'll scare her off.'

33

'Scare who off?' I say.

'Ellie,' she hisses.

'Who's Ellie?' I ask.

'Shhh,' says the girl again.

She throws the line into the water. 'I'm trying to catch squid,' whispers the girl. 'Ellie likes squid. If I dangle squid in the water, she might come and get it.' She turns to me and grins. 'Just imagine if we get to see her!'

Her eyes are sparkling in the moonlight. She looks excited. Either that or she's barking mad. At the moment, I'm betting on mad.

I try asking again. 'Who's Ellie?'

Something pulls on the fishing line.

'Shhh,' says the girl. She reels it in, and this time there really is a squid on the end of it.

'I've got one!' she hisses. She takes the squid off the hook, ties it to a bit of string and dangles it out the front of the boat. 'Now we wait,' she whispers as she sits, hunched, staring into the water.

This is turning into a

very weird

evening.

'Look,' I say, after a few minutes of waiting. 'I'm sure whatever you're doing is very important, but I've had a rotten evening. I've fallen down an outdoor loo and now I'm pretty sure I'm dying of cold. Would you mind if we rowed back to shore?'

'*SHHHH!*' hisses the girl. '*There!*'

She points out into the darkness, quivering with excitement.

Clearly this girl is as mad as a box of frogs.

Madder, even.

'Um . . . look,' I say, 'I don't mean to be rude, but . . .'

SPLASH!

And then I see it. A **huge** shadow, moving under the water, coming straight towards us.

'What is it?' I whisper.

But the girl doesn't answer. She grips the side of the boat, transfixed, as the shadow comes closer and closer.

Is it my sea monster? No, it's not the right shape. I can only just make it out, but this one's got a **long** neck. My monster's more like a mutant killer crocodile with giant jaws.

But there's certainly *some* sort of monster down there. It's **enormous**. As big as a whale. My heart starts thumping in my chest.

'It's her,' whispers the girl. 'It's really her . . .'

The shadow moves under the

boat, directly beneath us. The girl and I both lean over and peer into the murk below.

But right then the clouds move across the moon. The water turns black. All I can see is darkness. But it's still down there. It must be.

I wait for it to come charging up from underneath us, crashing into our tiny boat and SMASHING it into a thousand pieces. I wait and wait and wait for what seems like forever, clutching the side of the boat, knuckles white.

But nothing happens.

Finally the girl exhales. She's been holding her breath the whole time. I exhale too.

39

The girl slumps over. 'We were so close,' she mutters. 'So close.' She looks exhausted.

'What was it?' I whisper.

The girl looks at me. 'It was –'

CRUNCH!

Something does smash into us. The boat lurches upwards and we're both sent flying out into the lake.

SPLASH!

I tumble down into the freezing cold water. There are bubbles everywhere. I've no idea which way I'm facing.

SHOOP!

Something rushes past my face. A shiver shoots up my spine. But it's just one of the oars, sinking down to the bottom.

And then I hear it. A deep boom echoing through the water.

OOOOMAAAAaa

It's the same noise I heard in the toilet last night!

I start clawing my way up through the water, desperate to get to the surface. I'm just about to reach it when –

WHOOSH!

Something huge swims past me. Something the size of a double-decker bus.

OOOMAAAA it booms out again.

The force of it moving through the water throws me somersaulting backwards. And when I finally turn around it's gone, and all I can see is a huge fin **disappearing** into the depths. A fin the size of a surfboard.

I break the surface of the water and gasp, sucking in the air.

Amazingly, the boat's still the right way up. I pull myself into it, choking and wheezing, and collapse with a **soggy** thump onto the wooden deck.

'I knew it,' breathes the girl. She's lying next to me, staring up at the stars, eyes blazing. 'I knew she was real.'

'Who?' I gasp. 'What was that thing?'

The girl turns to face me. Her nose is a millimetre from mine. 'Ellie,' she says, 'the Loch Saurus monster.'

CHAPTER SIX
Endangered

'But what is the Loch Saurus monster?' I ask Molly.

That's the girl's name. We're back on shore, and she's invited me around for tea. Apparently she lives out in the swamp somewhere. It's almost one in the morning, which is a bit of an odd time for tea, but Molly doesn't seem to mind, and I'm far too $excited$ to go back to sleep.

'It's an elasmosaurus,' says Molly. 'That's why I call her Ellie.'

I can't believe it. 'An elasmosaurus? Are you sure?'

'Of course I'm sure,' says Molly. 'I know everything about dinosaurs.'

Ha! She obviously doesn't know as much as me.

'Elasmosauruses aren't dinosaurs,' I say. 'They're . . .'

'Plesiosaurs,' says Molly. 'I know.'

'Then why did you say dinosaurs?' I ask.

Molly grins. 'Because I was trying to make things simple for you. You're only little.'

How rude. I'm nine, and nine is NOT little. And I'm about to say so when Molly suddenly stops walking and

46

I bump straight into her.

'We're here,' she says.

'Here' is a **rusty** old caravan parked on bricks in a puddle.

'Is this really your house?' I ask.

'My dad can't afford a house,' says Molly.

'Why not?'

Molly shrugs. 'Because we haven't got much money.' She smiles. 'I don't mind, though. It's like being on a camping holiday all the time.'

We walk up the steps and open the door. It's really cosy inside. There are two big bunk beds up the back and a little kitchen in the middle. And there are photographs on the walls. Photographs of Saurus Lake. Some of the photos have **blurry** shapes in them.

'They're pictures of Ellie,' says Molly. 'I took them.'

I look closely at the pictures. One or two of the shapes do look a bit like an elasmosaurus. The same **long** neck, rising out of the water. I'm not certain, though. They could just be logs.

'Is tonight the closest you've got to Ellie?' I ask.

Molly nods. 'She almost took a squid two nights ago,' she says, 'but she's never come that close before. If we go out again tomorrow, we might just see her.'

'Wudya leek a biccie, laddie?'

A **shadow** looms over me. I look up. It's a huge man with a bright red beard and fierce black eyes, wearing

a skirt. He looks **ferocious**.

'That's my dad.' Molly smiles.
'He's asking if you'd like a biscuit.'

'Er . . . yes,' I say.
'That would be lovely.'

The enormous man stomps
away down the caravan.

'Why is he wearing a skirt?' I whisper.

Molly giggles. 'That's not a skirt, it's a kilt. Scottish men like to wear kilts.'

'Mulk o' tha coo?' **growls** Molly's dad, slamming a plate of biscuits down in front of me.

I stare at him, mouth open. What language is he speaking?

Molly leans over and whispers in my ear, 'He wants to know if you'd like a glass of milk.'

'Um . . . y-yes,' I stutter. 'Thank you.'

He nods and trudges off again. Molly's dad doesn't seem even a little bit surprised to have two children awake in his kitchen at one in the morning.

'So why is Ellie haunting my toilet?' I ask Molly, as I crunch on a biscuit.

'She's looking for food,' says Molly. 'There are too many people fishing on the lake, and she hasn't got enough to eat. And things are going to get worse. If the Parsnips build their fishing lodge, the whole lake will get fished out. Ellie will starve.'

'Why don't you tell someone about her?' I ask.

'I've tried,' she says, 'but no-one believes me. They all think I'm mad.'

I nod and look down at my hands. About an hour ago I thought she was mad too. But she isn't. Molly might be a bit **strange**, but there's nothing wrong with that.

'Now that you've seen Ellie,' says Molly, 'will you help me try to save her?'

She looks at me expectantly, but I don't need much convincing. Saving a plesiosaur sounds like my kind of adventure.

'Of course I will,' I say, 'but how do we do it?'

'All we need to do is prove she

53

exists,' Molly explains. 'Then Ellie will be protected, and the Parsnips won't be allowed to build anything. You can't make changes to an endangered animal habitat. And there's only one Ellie in the whole wide world. You can't get much more endangered than that.'

CHAPTER SEVEN
Meet the Parsnips

I wake up and look at the clock. It's six in the morning. I've only had four hours sleep. But I don't feel the tiniest bit tired. I'm far too *excited*.

I quietly put my clothes on. Pants, shirt, gumboots and a jacket. Then I tiptoe down the stairs, which is quite hard to do in gumboots.

'Grumpfle,' growls Grandad from his bedroom. He's just turning over, that's all. Grandad always says 'grumpfle' when he turns over in bed.

I sneak past the kitchen and open the back door. And there's Molly, already waiting for me.

'Let's go,' she whispers, passing me a fishing rod.

We start **squelching**
through the swamp towards the lake.

'So how long's Ellie been there?'
I ask Molly.

'I don't know,' she says. 'We only
moved to Saurus Street a month ago,
from Loch Ness in Scotland.'

I've heard of Loch Ness. Apparently

MONSTER

there's a

in that lake too. 'Did you ever see the
Loch Ness monster?' I ask.

'No,' she says, 'but I used to dream
about it every night. It's really strange.
The last time I dreamed about the Loch
Ness monster was the night we moved
to Saurus Street. And the next day I saw
Ellie!'

I nod. 'Maybe all lakes have got elasmosauruses.'

Molly shakes her head. 'Not all lakes,' she says. 'Only really mysterious ones.'

We reach the edge of Saurus Lake. It's covered in a thin layer of mist. There are tall trees growing on the bank, their tangled roots reaching into the murky water. Molly's right. It *is* **mysterious**.

'Climb aboard,' says Molly.

Her little fishing boat is tucked away behind a fern. She grabs a rope and pulls it out onto the water. We clamber aboard, and Molly starts rowing *slowly* through the mist. I can't believe I'm about to see a real live plesiosaur!

'Are you sure we're going to find her?' I ask.

'No,' admits Molly, 'but I reckon we've got a good chance. Elasmosauruses like to hunt in the mornings. And she's getting hungrier every day.'

'So what do we do?' I ask.

Molly reaches into her pocket and takes out a pot of worms. 'We start squidding,' she says.

But just as she's sharing out the worms, a **massive** white fishing boat roars towards us.

It swerves to a halt, soaking us with a wave of ice-cold water. So much for not getting wet.

'What are you two filthy little

urchins doing on my lake?' someone drawls.

It's Reverend Parsnip. He's standing at the front of his boat with his horrible wife, Priscilla. She's wearing a bright pink fishing jacket with **fluffy** buttons and a frilly collar. She looks ridiculous.

'This isn't your lake,' says Molly, hands on hips. Clearly she's not scared of Parsnips.

'It certainly is my lake,' drawls Reverend Parsnip. 'I bought it last week.'

'We're going to build a nice **big** fishing lodge here,' trills Priscilla, 'for nice wealthy tourists. And trailer trash like *you* won't be welcome.'

The Parsnips are the richest people on Saurus Street. They live in a massive mansion with an ocean view. They've got an enormous garden, a swimming

pool and a gigantic fountain. I know this because I sometimes peer through their **spiked** metal fence when Grandad takes me to the beach. But I've never been inside. No children have. There's a large yellow 'NO CHILDREN

ALLOWED' sign nailed to the fence.

'Now get off my lake,' snips Priscilla. 'You're scaring off my squid.' She pushes a button on her boat.

A huge fishing net starts rising out of the water. It's filled with hundreds of wriggling, **squiggling** squid.

Enough squid to feed an army.

'It's *you*,' says Molly. '*You're* the ones killing all the squid. *You're* the reason Ellie's got no food.'

'Who on earth is Ellie?' drawls Reverend Parsnip.

But just as he says it, Priscilla Parsnip starts to scream. Something's *rising* up out of the water.

I think he's about to find out who Ellie is.

CHAPTER EIGHT
Pull the Plug?

Ellie's head emerges from the water.

It's enormous, about two metres long. She's got bright green eyes and a mouth filled with *razor-sharp* teeth. Hopefully she likes eating Parsnips. Her head climbs up above the boats and just keeps on rising.

Whoa. Her neck is massive – it's

66

as long as a school bus! Pretty soon her head is way up high, staring down at us. Even the Parsnips' fishing boat looks tiny next to Ellie.

'Shoot it, Percival, shoot it!' squeals Priscilla Parsnip.

But Reverend Parsnip doesn't move. He just stands there, gawping, his mouth wide open.

'She's beautiful,' whispers Molly.

Molly's not wrong. Ellie is the most **amazing** thing I've ever seen.

A real live elasmosaurus. Wow. I have to pinch myself to make sure I'm awake.

Suddenly Ellie opens her mouth and starts bending down towards us.

I think someone's about to get eaten. But I'm wrong. She digs her teeth into the Parsnips' fishing net and rips it in two. Half the squid end up in

her mouth, and the other half tumble squiggling into the lake.

'My squid!' squeals Priscilla Parsnip.

Ellie takes no notice. With barely a ripple, she sinks down into the water, *twists* onto her side, flaps her massive flippers, and disappears into the depths.

Wow. That was truly awesome. I look at Molly. She's completely and utterly speechless.

But Priscilla Parsnip isn't. She starts wailing like a baby. 'There's a monster in my lake,' she **warbles**. 'I don't *want* a monster in my lake.'

'But, darling,' drawls the reverend, grabbing her by the shoulders, 'don't you realise what this means?'

69

He doesn't look upset. He's excited. Maybe he likes plesiosaurs too? Maybe he's not as bad as we thought?

'Yes!' shrills Priscilla Parsnip, pulling away from him. 'I know exactly what it means. It means that there's a horrid great monster in my lake. A big monster that's going to scare off all my tourists!'

'But, sweetness,' croons the reverend, 'don't you see? It's going to do exactly the opposite. Tourists will come from all over the world to see it! *And they'll pay whatever we ask!*'

Priscilla Parsnip pauses in her **blubbering**. She peers

at her husband. 'Whatever we ask?' she squeaks.

'Whatever we ask!' Her husband grins, hopping from foot to foot in excitement. 'We'll be millionaires!'

'And if it eats up all my fish,' trills Priscilla Parsnip, the colour returning to her cheeks, 'can we have it killed and stuffed and mounted in our lobby?'

'Yes, yes, yes!' crows the reverend. 'Of course we can! We'll be the envy of the world!'

Molly gasps. 'Hey!' she shouts. 'You can't kill Ellie. She's endangered!'

'So much the better!' Priscilla

Parsnip smirks, little white teeth peeking between her **puffy** pink lips. 'We'll be the only people in the world who've got one!' She cackles with glee, turns the boat around and the Parsnips race back towards the jetty.

Molly and I stand there, **frozen**. I don't know whether to laugh or cry. I've just seen a real live plesiosaur. And now the Parsnips are planning to hunt it down and stuff it.

They have got to be stopped.

Molly grabs the oars and starts rowing as hard as she can back to shore. She doesn't even wait for me to sit down. I almost tumble into the water.

'What are we going to do?' I ask, as

I regain my **bal**a**nce**.

She turns to look at me. I've never ever seen anyone look so determined.

'The only thing we can do,' Molly says. 'We're going to pull the plug.'

CHAPTER NINE
Operation Meteor

As soon as we reach the shore, Molly leaps out of the boat and starts running into the **swamp**. I don't know where she's going, but wherever it is it's in the wrong direction. There's nothing that way. It's just an overgrown marsh filled with *tangled* weeds and rubbish.

'This is stupid,' I call, running after Molly. 'Where are we going? We need to come up with a plan.'

'We *have* got a plan,' she shouts back. 'We're going to pull out the plug.'

'Pull out the plug?' I say, ducking under a branch. 'What do you mean "pull out the plug"? It's a *lake*, not a bathtub.'

'I know,' says Molly, 'but it's still got a plug.'

She's being **ridiculous**. I've half a mind to stop running and turn back. I've got to do something to help. I can hear Reverend Parsnip shouting orders back at the lake. He's sending other boats out. They're going to look for Ellie.

'We haven't got time for this,' I shout at Molly. 'We need to come up with a plan. A *sensible* plan.'

Molly spins around. 'This *is* a sensible plan,' she says. 'We're going to *pull* the plug out of the lake and let Ellie swim out to sea. That way she can escape.'

I roll my eyes at her. 'For the last time, Molly, *lakes don't have plugs*!'

76

'Well, what do you call *that*, then?' she asks. She drags me through a thorny bush and points.

And there it is. The plug.

In front of us is a gully, **OVERGROWN** with weeds.

At one end of the gully there's water. Lots of water. It's the end of the outlet

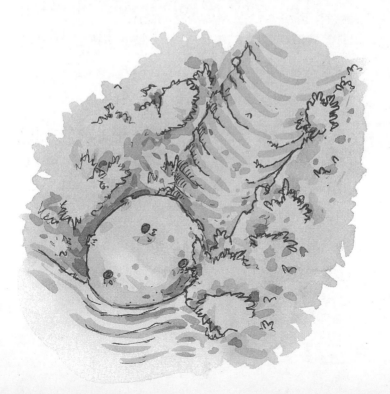

that leads from the lake. At the other end of the gully is a dry riverbed. And slap bang in the middle of that riverbed is an enormous rock covered in craters.

I've never seen anything like it before. The surface of the rock is smooth and shiny. It looks like it might've come from another planet. And it's **enormous**.

The rock is completely blocking the water, keeping it in the lake. If the gully wasn't so overgrown, you'd see the rock from miles away.

I clamber down into the gully. The rock looms right over my head. I reach out to touch it. Maybe it's a spaceship?

Maybe there are aliens inside? **Weird** blue ones with eyes in their foreheads?

'What is it?' I whisper.

'It's a meteor,' says Molly, 'a flying rock from outer space.'

Wow. That rates about an eight out of ten on my Awesomeness Scale. The only thing that's ever rated higher was Ellie. I'm having a very awesome morning.

'Is this the meteor that wiped out the dinosaurs?' I ask.

'Of course not,' says Molly. 'That one was much bigger. This one fell more recently. Maybe a million years ago. It **plugged** up the river and turned it into a lake.'

Cool. Imagine having a meteor for a plug? That would make bath times way more exciting.

'So what are we going to do?' I ask.

'Move it,' says Molly.

I stare at the meteor. It's so big it's almost blocking out the sun. 'Er . . . and how would we do that, then?'

Molly looks at me. 'With a really, really big **BANG**.'

CHAPTER TEN
The Big Bang

The Big Bang, or as I like to call it, the

FANTASTIC SPACE KAPOW,

was the biggest bang there's ever been. It sent rocks and lumps and bits flying all over the universe. Some of those rocks grouped together and turned into planets. Some stayed really hot

and turned into suns. But other rocks just stayed being rocks, and spent their time *flying* around visiting different galaxies. These rocks are called meteors. And *sometimes* these meteors, which never look where they're going, fly straight into planets. And about a million years ago, that's how our meteor **crashed** into Earth.

The Big Bang sent the meteor to Earth, and we're going to need a Big Bang to send it back again. And for once I know exactly what to do.

Molly and I have split up. She's gone back to her caravan and I've gone back to Granny and Grandad's house. We're on a mission, and we don't have much time.

I look around the house. I need to
find things beginning with T.

I start in my bedroom.
Tinsel, T-shirts, Transformers,
a tambourine and a toy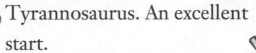
Tyrannosaurus. An excellent
start.

I put them all in a bin
liner and run into the bathroom.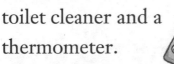
Toothpaste, tablets, toe cream,
toilet cleaner and a
thermometer.
Brilliant. I pile
them on top
and run
DOWNSTAIRS.

It's the kitchen next. I open the cupboard and see what's in there. Turmeric, tofu, tea bags and Tabasco spicy sauce. I take them all and throw in some tongs for good measure.

I look in my bag to see what I've got. There are a lot of things beginning with T, but I'm not sure it's enough. I might need some help.

I can hear **banging**

in the sitting room. I run through the door, and there's Grandad hammering wooden planks over the windows.

'Grandad?' I say.

He spins around. 'Ah,' he says, 'it's you, boy. I thought I'd been flanked by

84

the enemy!' Grandad's wearing his old army uniform, and he's got an army helmet on his head. 'I'm just preparing our defences,' he adds.

Good old Grandad. The Parsnips won't be taking this house without a **fight**.

'Grandad,' I ask, 'where do we keep things beginning with T?'

'A cup of tea?' says Grandad. 'Excellent idea. One must keep one's fluids up before a battle. My army flask is in the shed.'

The shed! I haven't looked in there yet.

I run outside, push up the roller door, and see what I can find. Turpentine and Toad Repellent. They look good. I empty them into the bag.

And there's something else **hidden** behind all the paints. Tapioca mix. It must be one of Granny's homemade cooking recipes. Grandad's stuck a sticky note on it: *Highly flammable*. I've no idea what that means, but it begins with T, so into the bag it goes. I think that might just be enough.

'Bye, Grandad!' I shout, as I hurry around the house.

I race as *fast* as I can back to the meteor. There's lots of activity out on the lake now. I can see big motorboats with harpoons and nets.

They're probably using sonar devices to track Ellie down. The kind that **bounce** sounds off the bottom of the lake to see what's down there (a bit like how bats use sound to see what's around them – 'echolocation', I think it's called. I learnt about it in science class.) They're bound to find Ellie using sonar. We need to hurry up.

When I finally reach the meteor, Molly's already there.

'Did you find anything?' I ask.

'Loads of things,' she says.

She opens her bag and I peer inside. Nuts, nachos, napkins, nappies, noodles, nail varnish and nasal decongestant.

All things beginning with N. Exactly what we need.

I nod. 'We're good to go,' I say.

We carry our bags over to the meteor. 'Are you sure this is going to work?' asks Molly.

'Certain,' I say. 'I was told about it by an expert.'

And that's true. There's a big kid at school who knows all about **explosives**. His name is Spud. He gave me the formula ages ago.

'All right,' I say. 'We need to do this quickly. As soon as everything mixes together, it's going to explode.'

We hold up our bags, ready to tip.

'I hope no-one catches us,' says Molly.

'They won't,' I say. 'They're all out on the lake. No-one knows we're here.'

And just as I say this a hand

grabs me.

'That,' drawls the owner of the hand, 'is where you'll find you're wrong.'

CHAPTER ELEVEN
Tapioca Surprise

I turn around. Reverend Parsnip is sneering at me down his long, thin nose. He looks as if he's trodden in something **smelly**.

'Why aren't you out on the lake?' I squeak.

'Because I am rich,' says Reverend Parsnip, 'and I can pay other people

to do my dirty work for me.' He leans closer. 'Which gives me time to keep an eye on meddlesome children like you.'

My breath feels frozen in my lungs. But we have to act. There's no time to lose.

'Quick,' I whisper to Molly. 'Do it. Do it now!'

Reverend Parsnip tries to pull me away, but he's too **slow**. I empty my bag onto the meteor. Molly does the same. I wait for the explosion.

But nothing happens. It all just mixes together and **gloops** down onto the ground.

Reverend Parsnip pushes past me and bends over to stare at the mess. 'What are you disgusting little creatures up to?' he drawls.

There's no point pretending. 'TNT,' I say.

'What?' he snaps, peering around at me.

'TNT,' I repeat. 'The most **POWERFUL** explosive there is. We're sending the meteor back into space.' I try to look confident, but I'm starting to feel a bit silly.

Reverend Parsnip narrows his eyes. 'TNT?' he asks.

'Yes,' I say, 'TNT. A big kid told me how to make it.'

A mean little smile appears on

Reverend Parsnip's face. 'And what exactly did he tell you?' he drawls.

'Well, it's obvious,' I say, feeling less and less sure of myself. 'Things beginning with T mixed with things beginning with N, mixed with more things beginning with T.'

Reverend Parsnip's smile spreads into a grin. And then, very, very slowly he starts to laugh.

'Haw haw haw,' he chortles. He points a **bony** finger at the mess on the ground. 'You think *that* is how you make TNT?'

I can feel my face going red. 'We even added t-t-tapioca mix,' I stutter, 'and that's fler-mam-able!'

'HAW HAW HAW!' cackles Reverend Parsnip. 'Fler-mam-able! HA HA HA! *Fler-mam-able! HEE HEE –*'

KABOOOOOOOM!

All three of us are thrown backwards. The whole world turns into sound and light. I look up. The meteor is screaming its way up into the sky, a trail of fire *blazing* behind it.

It worked. *It actually worked!* We've sent the meteor back to space!

'Molly,' I shout, turning to look at her. 'We did it!'

But Molly doesn't answer.

She's looking towards the lake, her face as white as a sheet.

'What?' I say. 'What is it?'

But she just points, her eyes wide with **fear**.

I turn around. Oh. There's a wall of water thundering towards us. A wall of water nine metres high.

I'm not sure I thought this plan through as well as I should've.

CHAPTER TWELVE
The Great Flood

Reverend Parsnip screams a high-pitched scream that almost **BURSTS** my eardrums.

Molly reaches out and takes my hand. 'It was great knowing you,' she says.

I turn to her. 'It was nice knowing you too,' I whisper.

The wall of water rushes closer and closer. Reverend Parsnip disappears in an instant, his scream cut horribly short. I close my eyes and wait for the water to reach us.

WHOOOOOSH!

The water hits me like a truck. I'm sent flying, water flooding up my nose and into my mouth.

I open my eyes. I'm completely surrounded. I don't know whether I'm facing up or down, left or right. All around me is rushing, ROARING, racing water.

I can feel Molly clinging tightly to my hand. And I'm clinging tightly right

back. She's trying to say something but she can't make a sound. It doesn't matter though. There's nothing we can do. The water's too strong.

SWOOP!

Something enormous sweeps underneath us. Something **huge** and *fast* and powerful. And all of a sudden we're rushing upwards through the water and towards the light.

GASP!

I take a breath, sucking the air into my lungs. I'm on the surface. I made it! I survived!

'Thomas! *Thomas!*' It's Molly. She's got her arms around my waist. And she's

screaming into my ear. 'It's Ellie,' she yells. *'She's saved us!'*

I look down. And my heart almost stops.

We're riding on the back of a mighty elasmosaurus!

I'm sitting on Ellie's shoulders, her four gigantic flippers beating the surrounding water. Her neck, which must be five metres long, stretches out in front of me. Her skin is blue and green, the colours rippling and

shimmering

in the shining sun. She's the most incredible thing I've ever seen.

'YAHOOOOO!' yells Molly.

I look behind me. The whole swamp is flooded. Lake Saurus is rushing down into the gully. It's *swirling* around in a gigantic whirlpool as it surges down towards us. I can see the fishing boats spinning and tipping in the water.

'Your grandad's house!' shouts

101

Molly. 'We're heading straight for it!'

I turn back around. She's right. The water's rushing straight towards it. Oh no! It's going to get **flattened**!

The water gushes through the back door. I wait for the house to be torn apart. But it isn't. The water bursts through the front door, the house leans to the left and, with a creak and a groan, it rises to the surface of the water. Granny and Grandad are afloat!

'TALLY-HO!' booms Grandad. He's leaning out of the upstairs window, army helmet sparkling in the sun. 'Hoist the anchor!' he shouts. 'Raise the mainsail. The SS *Saurus* is away!'

With a CRASH of splintering wood, the house smashes through the

front fence and starts sailing down Saurus Street. Ellie comes racing after it, *speeding* through the water like a missile.

'Morning, Mrs Wilcott!' shouts Grandad.

I look to my left. Old Mrs Wilcott is standing on her front step in fluffy slippers, gawping at us.

'Don't forget to put your rubbish bin out!' yells Grandad. 'It's collection day tomorrow.'

The water starts moving faster and faster. It's building up into a **mighty** wave. The residents of Saurus Street stand dumbstruck on their doorsteps as we thunder past, the surging water sweeping up cars as we go.

Suddenly I hear a weak shout from behind us.

'Darling, please! Pull me up!'

The unmistakable drawl of Reverend Parsnip. I twist my head around. The Parsnips' fishing boat is roaring up towards us.

Reverend Parsnip is clinging to the side, desperately trying to climb back into the boat. But his wife isn't slowing down. She's hunched over the wheel, eyes **bulging**, lips white, bright pink fishing suit torn and tatty.

Priscilla Parsnip has come back for revenge.

CHAPTER THIRTEEN
The Real Loch Saurus Monster

'You wrecked my lake!' squawks Priscilla Parsnip. She guns her boat towards us.

Ellie flaps her flippers and surges forward, but the fishing boat is too fast.

Priscilla Parsnip is getting closer and closer. I can see all the little red lines squiggling around in her eyeballs.

'You freed my squid,' she squeals, shaking her **bony** pink fist at us. *'You stole my monster!'*

Priscilla Parsnip grabs a fishing rod and wedges it behind the wheel to stop it from moving. Then she starts lurching towards the front of the boat.

She's clutching something. I think it's a harpoon gun.

'Darling!' whines Reverend Parsnip. 'Please! Slow the boat down. I can't climb up . . .' He's desperately trying to stretch his leg over the side, but it keeps slipping off.

'I should *never* have listened to you.' snaps Priscilla Parsnip, **spinning** around to look at him. 'We were far too kind to these people. We should have knocked down their houses and evicted them from Saurus Street. *We should have had them arrested!*'

'But, sweet pea,' wails the reverend, 'it's over now. There's nothing we can do. The fishing lodge is finished!'

'IT'S NOT OVER TILL I SAY IT IS!' shrieks Priscilla Parsnip. 'We invested every penny we own into that fishing lodge. And I WANT . . . THAT . . . MONSTER!' She reaches the front of the boat. She looks completely **crazed**.

Grabbing the harpoon gun she

points it straight at us. She starts squeezing the trigger. I grit my teeth and wait for the harpoon to strike . . .

GRRRUEEEEERRRRR.

Priscilla Parsnip *freezes*. There's a sound coming from beneath the water. A sound so deep it makes the air shake.

'What was that?' I ask Molly. 'Another elasmosaurus?'

But it can't be. It didn't sound like Ellie. It sounded bigger, and louder, and scarier.

GRRRUEEEERRRR.

Something huge rises from the water behind the Parsnips' boat. Something terrifying. Its eyes appear first, and then its gigantic snout, and

112

then the rest of its **humungous**
body. It roars again.

My tummy turns upside down.
I can't believe it. It really exists. It's the
hideous green water monster from my
nightmares.

'It's a kronosaurus,' gasps Molly.

CHAPTER FOURTEEN

Ginger Snaps

With one mighty bite the kronosaurus crushes the boat, and the Parsnips are sent screaming and flailing into the swirling water.

But the kronosaurus doesn't stop to eat them. It's got its eyes on bigger prey. It whips its monstrous tail and rushes

towards us, sweeping the debris aside.

'That must be why Ellie swam up your outdoor loo,' yells Molly. 'She wasn't looking for food. She was trying to escape THAT!'

The kronosaurus thunders towards us, getting closer and closer.

'We need to go faster!' I shout.

The kronosaurus 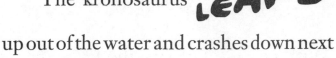 **LEAPS**

up out of the water and crashes down next to us. Its jaws snap closed centimetres from my head.

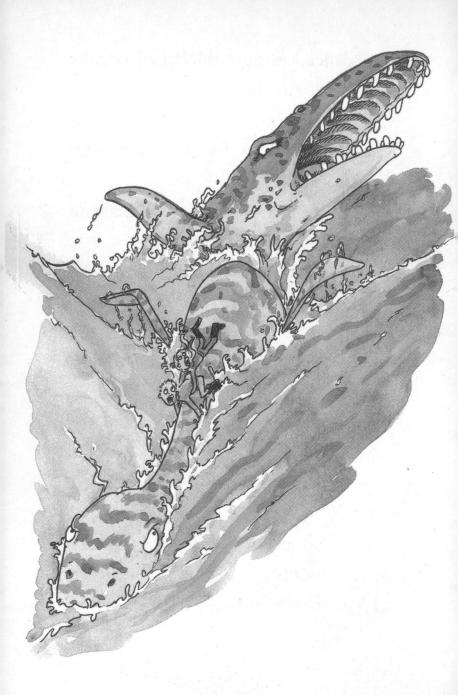

'Quick,' shouts Molly, 'into the house!'

'What?' I splutter.

'*The house!*' she repeats. '*Go into the house!*'

I think she wants me to steer. I'm not quite sure how you steer a plesiosaur, but there's never been a better time to try. I push Ellie's neck to the left. And it works! She twists around and *accelerates* towards the house.

'Go through the back door,' shouts Molly. 'The kronosaur will be too big to fit.'

I reckon *we're* going to be too big to fit, but we've got to try something. The kronosaurus is right behind us. It's just about to strike! Ellie flicks her tail and speeds through the back door.

Thankfully, she's slim enough to fit.

'There,' says Molly. 'We lost it.'

CRUNCH!

No we didn't. The kronosaurus smashes through the doorframe and charges after us.

'FASTER!' yells Molly.

We race down the passage, the kronosaurus closing in.

'Turn right!' shrieks Molly.

We crash into the bathroom. The sink bobbles past us, my Spider-Man toothbrush bobbing up and down beside it.

'I think someone must have left the tap on,' says Granny. She's right in front of us, floating around in the bathtub, knitting a scarf. 'But don't worry,' she adds. 'I'm sure Grandad's called the plumber.'

The kronosaurus bursts through the wall behind us, mouth wide open.

'Quick, Granny!' I shout. 'Jump!'

I grab Granny's arm and pull her
onto Ellie's back. And just in time! The

monster's jaws **crunch**
closed, crushing the bathtub into tiny
pieces.

'How rude,' tuts Granny. 'That was
an antique.'

Suddenly everything lurches to the

left. The kronosaurus crashes through the side of the house, Ellie crunching after it.

'It's the water,' shouts Molly. 'It's reaching the bottom of Saurus Street. The wave's about to break!'

She's right. We're thundering steeply down towards the sea. The water is building up into a massive tidal wave, 30 metres high. Cars, trees and bits of boat are swirling all around us.

We're right at the tip of the wave, and we're just about to **smash** down into the ocean far below.

'What do we do now?' yells Molly.

I look behind us. The kronosaurus is still closing in. It's not giving up. Its huge jaws are opening wide. We've got nowhere left to go.

'Ginger snap?' asks Granny.

She holds out a cake tin. She must have had it hidden under her knitting. It's full of homemade ginger snaps.

Granny's ginger snaps! I've had them before. They're **volcanic!** They make the tapioca mix look like treacle tart!

'I'll take the whole tin!' I shout.

Granny grins. She loves it when
people appreciate her cooking.

'AAAAAARGH!' shrieks Molly.

The kronosaurus is centimetres

away. Its jaws are **open wide**!

'Try some of these!' I yell. And I throw the whole tin down the kronosaurus's throat.

There's a gulp as it swallows them. And then a gurgle and a hiss. Smoke starts steaming from its nostrils. The kronosaurus closes its mouth. Its tummy bulges. It doesn't look too happy.

BOOM!

The kronosaurus explodes. And wow, what a blast! The whole wave erupts in an avalanche of water, noise and kronosaurus bits. We're sent flying into the air.

'HOLD ON!' shouts Molly. She grabs hold of my hand. I grab hold of Granny's hand.

'YIPPEE!' hoots Granny. She's having a marvellous time.

WHOAAAA! We somersault upside down. We're tumbling down towards the road. We're about to go

SPLAT.

Then something spins past us. It's Grandad's house!

'Take my hand!' Grandad's leaning out of the upstairs window, army hat still perched on his head.

Molly reaches out and grabs his hand. And all together we start spiralling down and down and down towards Saurus Street.

CHAPTER FIFTEEN
Nice Soft Landing

We land on top of something with a deafening crunch. The whole house **shudders** and shakes, but it stays together. It might be old, but it's sturdy.

We all clamber up through the window and into the house.

'Where are we?' asks Molly.

I look around. We've landed in the middle of a huge garden with hedgerows, flowerbeds and a **gigantic** fountain. Running around the edge of it is a **spiked** iron fence. I'm sure I recognise it.

Grandad bursts out laughing. 'Well, they wanted our house removed,' he giggles. 'And removed is what they got!'

And that's when I realise. We've landed in the Parsnips' garden. I look around. 'But where is the Parsnips' house?'

Molly starts laughing too. 'We've landed on top of it!' she says.

I lean out the window and look down. And there are the remains of Castle Parsnip, crushed flat underneath us.

Something falls out of the sky and lands with a thump next to us.

It's Molly's caravan. The door opens and a drenched Scotsman staggers out.

'Well, tha' woz a wee bit wet,' he says, wringing the water from his kilt.

All of a sudden Molly grabs my hand and gasps. 'Look, there she goes! She made it!' She points out towards the sea.

The last of Lake Saurus is washing down into the ocean. And there, looping through the water, is an enormous plesiosaur, pale blue skin shining in the sun. Ellie really is *magnificent*.

'OOOOMAAAAaa,'

she calls, as she dives beneath the waves.

I smile. It almost sounds like she's saying my name.

CHAPTER SIXTEEN
A Room with a View

I wake up and look at the clock. It's midnight.

The witching hour.

The wind is whistling through the trees and the house is creaking and groaning like a ghost. I creep over to my window and peer outside.

I like our new garden. It's

beautiful. There's a maze of sunflowers, a swimming pool and a brand new outdoor loo, tucked behind a hedge in the shape of a dragon.

And there are no witches. Or werewolves. Or water monsters. They're not welcome here.

I like my new neighbours too. Molly comes around to play every

day, and sometimes her dad visits too.
He and Grandad have become the
best of friends. Molly's dad even likes
Granny's cooking. 'Good strong stuff,'
he calls it.

But most of all I like the view.
From my bedroom window I can see

the waves rolling away towards the horizon, and the moon shining down on the water.

And sometimes, if I look really hard, I can see something else. Something far out to sea. A long thin neck rising out of the water.

Of course, it might not be a neck. It might just be a log, or the mast of an old wooden fishing boat. Or it could just be my **imagination**.

But I think I know what it really is.

135

SAURUS STREET

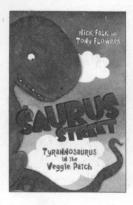

NICK FALK and TONY FLOWERS

TYRANNOSAURUS IN THE Veggie Patch

NICK FALK and TONY FLOWERS

A PTERODACTYL STOLE MY HOMEWORK

NICK FALK and TONY FLOWERS

THE VERY NAUGHTY VELOCIRAPTOR

Saurus Street is just like any other street . . . except for the dinosaurs.

Collect them all!

Watch out for
Billy is a Dragon
by Nick Falk
and Tony Flowers
coming in March 2014

Loved the book?

There's so much more
stuff to check out online